ALSO BY JILL SHEELEY

The World According to Fraser

THE WORLD
ACCORDING TO
Fraser
A MEMOIR

 by FRASER
with JILL SHEELEY

Illustrated by BILL SCHORR

ISBN-10: 0-9609108-9-1
ISBN-13: 978-0-9609108-9-2
Copyright © 2006, by Jill Sheeley
First printing 2006

COURTNEY PRESS · P.O. Box 845 · Aspen, Colorado 81612 · www.jillsheeleybooks.com

Printed in USA

Disclaimer: The adventure stories Jill wrote about Fraser are for children.
Fraser's memoir is intended for people and dogs of all ages. There are a few words and
descriptions that an adult may want to omit before reading it to their children. RATED: PG13

Partial proceeds will benefit the new Aspen Animal Shelter.

I dedicate my book to my mentor, Abby.
She taught me so much
and I'm forever grateful.

—FRASER

I dedicate this book to all the dogs
who are or have been in my life.
They bring me such joy, loyalty,
companionship, and most of all, love:
Fraser, Maggie, Abby, Scout,
Chief, Killy and Brandy.

—JILL SHEELEY

CONTENTS

ACKNOWLEDGMENTS

We would like to express our gratitude to the many people who helped make this book a reality:

To our family—Don and Courtney for your input, patience and understanding.

Thanks for all the great runs, treats, balls thrown, pets, love and for understanding my fear of thunderstorms this summer— Fraser.

Bland, Michael and "the girls"—for your hospitality and love.

Rosemary—my wonderful vet who makes sure I'm healthy.

Bill Schorr—an incredible cartoonist who
really brought my story to life!

To those who gave advice—Amy, Mark, Bland,
Muffy, Susan, Allison, Shelley, Jon, James,
Gwyn, Laura, Ed, Ruth and Don.

To Susan—thanks for proofing again and
again!

Marjorie DeLuca—for your creativity. You're
an amazing designer, a magician with your
computer and a delight to work with.

Special thanks to Hensley Peterson—an
empathetic and extraordinary editor who
jumped in and helped every day, always
with a smile and great enthusiasm.

Properly trained,
a man can be dog's best friend.

—COREY FORD

INTRODUCTION

I'm writing my life's story because (and I don't mean to brag) I'm a celebrity and from what I've heard, lots of people seem interested. No, I'm not the TV star, "Frasier." In fact our names aren't even pronounced or spelled the same. TV's fine, but I'm an outdoors kind-of-a-guy. Real live adventures are my shtick. It's all my human mom's fault—she wrote children's books about my adventures and they sold like hotcakes. I felt it was about time to tell "all" and pass on what I've learned. Feel free to read my entire story or a chapter at a time. If you'd like, skip around. You might enjoy my column, "Just Ask Fraser," where dogs of all shapes and sizes get answers to their puzzling and heartfelt questions. The entire family will be challenged with my True or False quiz. There's something for everyone in my book.

I'm patiently waiting for a movie to be made about my adventures. Go for it fellow Lab actors. I hope it's produced soon as I'm getting up there in dog years and would be tickled pink to see myself on the silver screen. I love air conditioned movie theatres and doggie popcorn. I'd even look forward to signing "paw-tographs" on promotional posters after the premier showing.

Yesterday I was a dog.
Today I'm a dog.
Tomorrow I'll probably still be a dog.
Sigh!
There's so little hope
for advancement.

—CHARLES M. SCHULZ
(1922–2000)

> *"I think dogs are the most amazing creatures; they give unconditional love. For me they are the role model for being alive."*
>
> —GILDA RADNER

THE BEGINNING

L et me introduce myself. My name is Fraser. I'm a large yellow Labrador retriever—actually, a red-blooded Canine American. I weigh over 100 pounds and according to my owners, I have big, beautiful, very kind eyes. You might even say they are movie star eyes.

I was born in Kansas in 1994 and was taken from my real mother one sad day in early spring. My ten brothers and sisters and I couldn't figure out what we'd done wrong. One minute we were one big family happily sucking on our mother's milk-filled

I haven't
heard from
my mom yet.

teats, and the next minute we were thrown into a large vehicle and driven into the mountains of Colorado. Since I've never heard from my mother, I sometimes have abandonment issues. However, I've adapted well and am thriving.

My brothers and sisters and I were driven by a nice lady named Debby to her dog grooming shop in Aspen, Colorado. We had passed our tiny puppy stage and were into our two-month-old phase of life. Basically, we were more energetic, animated and curious. We were becoming increasingly socialized and growing like wildflowers. Over the years, I've come to find out I was properly weaned, so I thank my dear sweet mother.

Life was easy. We were on a tight schedule. We woke up at 6:00 A.M. and Debby would take us all out to relieve ourselves; puppy chow at 6:30 A.M.; a short nap; a drink of water; and into Debby's car at 7:30 A.M. for a long drive to her shop, "Tailwagger's." Yes, we ate, slept, drank and went outside to play. Every once in awhile someone would show up and talk baby-talk to us. Each one of us would get picked up and cuddled. The people would talk about each and every part of us: "Oh, look at his paws, he's going to be huge." And to my sister, "This one is sooooo cute." And so forth. All we really wanted to do was either play or go back to sleep. But the people stayed a long time critiquing us.

Then one day, a blond-haired man and a brown-haired lady came along and took one look at me—I must have looked particularly handsome—and told Debby they wanted me. I wasn't prepared to leave my brothers and sisters, but the next thing I knew, the lady had me in her arms waving my paw goodbye to my family.

It all happened so fast. They drove me up a mountain road to a log house and placed me on a nice comfy piece of rug. Hey, this was kind of nice. I had two big teddy bears around me and five or six puppy toys in a little box. They gave me a yummy treat and I went right to sleep.

When I woke up, the blond-haired man lifted me up in his arms and told me all about how his Irish setter had died recently. I listened and was so sad I almost started crying. I decided then and there I'd be the best companion ever. I guess you could say we bonded. He set me down and along came a large sable-colored collie dog. The blond-haired man said to me, "Meet Abby." He started petting her and telling her that I'm the newest member of the family.

The man left me alone with Abby. She sniffed me a few times and then started licking me all over. She didn't smell like my mother, but she seemed to

My first
encounter
with Scratchy

be taking over the role. She laid down on the rug and I fell asleep right next to her soft stomach. From that day on, I quit missing my real mom.

I woke up hours later to a hissing sound and a big, black cat staring at me. Abby was nowhere in sight so I jumped up and put up my paws to say, "Hi." This cat was like, "Are you kidding? I'm here to show you who's the boss." So, she hissed and put out her sharp claws. I think she wanted to hurt me.

"No, Scratchy, no," the brown-haired lady yelled as she ran down the stairs. She grabbed me up into her arms and if I were a cat, I'd have started purring. I felt so safe. She baby-talked me until I settled down. She told me that Scratchy was a wonderful cat and that we'd be friends in no time. WHEW. I wasn't real keen on waking up every day to hissing and a mean cat-face baring her teeth at me.

A horn was honking in the distance and when the car stopped, a little girl flew out and pulled me from the brown-hair lady's arms. "Oh, Mom," she said, "you and Dad got a new puppy. He's so cute. What's his name?"

"We haven't named him yet. Start thinking of names and by Sunday, we'll decide. You can help," she said.

The little girl put me down and started running around me. We played and played until I was so tired I fell asleep on the grass.

The entire week, all I kept hearing were names, names and more names. *Dock* was repeated over and over as was *Pier, Marina, Cleat, Mooring, Anchor, Star, Sailor, Laser* and *Jib*. Turns out my new family likes to sail—duh. Since I didn't have a name yet, they all called me "pup" or "sweetie" or "lambie" or "cutie pie." Speaking of names, what was I supposed to call my new family? The lady with the brown hair was called "Mom" by the little girl and the blond-haired man was called "Dad." So that's what I call them now. My mom and dad call the little girl "Courtney" so I, too, refer to her by that name.

One sunny, windy day, my family and I drove in an open jeep to a lake. They put me on their sailboat and my mom held me in her arms as we sailed. I'd just start to fall asleep when my mom would get up and move to the other side of the boat. My dad would yell, "Coming about, hard to lee," and then I'd know it was time to wake up and we'd move again. This sailing game was really tiring for me. I got wet and the wind in my face made me want to sleep. When we finally quit, I played in the sand and chewed on my new toy, a rubber, squeaky duck.

Fraser
~~SAILOR~~
~~ANCHOR~~
~~DOCK~~
~~JIB~~

I finally
have a
name!

Next thing I knew, we were driving down the road and my mom, dad and Courtney got real excited. My dad suddenly stopped the jeep and said, "I've got it. Let's name him *Fraser* after our good friend in New Zealand."

"I love that name," said my mom. "Fraser's a stud and someday this pup will be a stud, too."

"That's it," they said together, "We'll name him Fraser." And that's how, on a windy day, I got my name.

"One reason a dog is such a loveable creature is his tail wags instead of his tongue."

—UNKNOWN

CRUISING THE NEIGHBORHOOD

Life was better than I could ever have expected. Living in the mountains is the very best. I have tons of land to run and a cool pond in the front yard to swim. Now that I'm older and my family trusts me with Abby, they leave us home alone while they go to work and Courtney goes to school. Abby spends a little time trying to train me, but gives up quickly. I rub my paws together and go on my neighborhood route.

First, I run up the hill to Kathryn's house. She is always throwing balls to Bill, a Jack Russell terrier.

She greets me with a small, bite-size biscuit and Bill and I chase balls together until I'm so tired (Bill never gets tired of the almighty ball), I go into their house and take a long nap. When I wake up, I go outside in time to watch Kathryn and Bill leave in their car. I'm left alone. I run down the hill and check in with Abby, who's *like*, "Okay—fine, Fraser, you're cool. You can leave again—I'm ready for my nap." So I do.

Next I trot up the main hill and go for a run with my best friends, Bo and Lady, two big golden retrievers. Their mom and dad join us, which is great because they throw us tennis balls galore. Instead of going home, I stop along the way at a really nice house. No one is home, but I know how to go in the doggie door. I also know where they stash the biscuits. There's a real comfy couch in the living room, so I jump up and lay between two really soft pillows.

I'm so tired that when the owner, a nice doctor, comes into the living room; I barely lift up my sleepy head. "Hi, Fraser," he greets me, "I'd better call your mom to come and get you so she doesn't worry."

Next thing I know, my mom and Courtney are at the door. Courtney picks me up but my mom is busy apologizing to the good doctor. I can't figure

Hello...
I'm here!

out why my mom is so mad at me. She hardly ever is.

After my dinner, I'm napping but I hear my mom and dad discussing my recent behavior: "We're just going to have to either take him to work," said my mom. "Or, he'll have to stay in his pen," said my dad.

Gosh dog it, my days of freedom and making myself at home at other people's houses has come to an abrupt end—at least for awhile.

"No matter how little money and how few
possessions you own, having a dog makes you rich."
—LOUIS SABIN

FAME AND FORTUNE

I 've been living the dog's life for four luxurious years. I've been fed, cleaned up after, exercised several times a day, played with, sweet talked, petted, massaged and I've chased thousands of balls—my days are full and happy. What more could a guy ask for?

When life seems too good to be true, well sometimes that's so. My mom, dad and I were out one day for a mountain bike ride and they were discussing this idea my mom had about writing a kids' book—about none other than ME. I really have no idea what this "entails" so I just kept running and sniffing. She told my dad: "There are no children's books about Aspen for kids. My favorite book when I was growing up was *Lassie*." My dad said his favorite book was *Big Red*. Before Abby and I came along, he owned a slew of Irish setters because he loved the dog, Big Red.

"Kids need heroes," my mom said. "Fraser's our hero." I hang onto her every word and start prancing—wow, really, I'm their hero?! "Remember when Fraser saved Lucy from that snow bank?" asked my mom. Lucy was a really old, teeny, tiny white Poodle. One day, on one of my daily walks I heard an older lady yelling Lucy's name. Somehow Lucy had gotten herself off the beaten trail and was stuck in deep snow and couldn't get out. The older lady couldn't help her. No big deal. I ran up to where they were, broke through the deep, heavy snow, dug Lucy out with my large paws and ran back and forth several times to make her a path. She simply followed me down the path to the waiting arms of her owner. I

Really, guys,
I'm YOUR hero?

thought it was a blast! I especially enjoyed the treats the lady gave me and all the nice pets and sweet words of praise. Turns out she was so grateful, she called my family that night and told them the story. Even Abby was impressed, which is quite a feat.

"And remember when Fraser saved that little girl from drowning in our pond?" asked my dad. One summer evening I was just returning from a walk when I heard a noise coming from our pond. At first I thought it might be a duck, but turns out it was a little girl who couldn't swim. She started beating the water and then began to go under. Instinctively, I swam next to her and let her grab onto me as I swam to shore. I heard our neighbors yelling, "Callie, Callie, oh my God." They carried bright flashlights and ran over to her with blankets. They seemed very happy to see her. "What happened?" they asked.

"I slipped on some mud by the side of the pond and fell in," she said. "I was so scared, but then that dog pulled me to safety. He appeared out of nowhere," she replied.

I was glad the girl was okay, but I was really hungry so I ran home.

The next day my mom told me I saved the little girl's life. The neighbors and their friends dropped off a huge basket filled with treats and toys for me. Of course, I shared with Abby, but it sure was nice to be rewarded.

My mom and dad kept exchanging my "heroic" stories all the way up a very steep hill. My mom chatted a mile a minute about this book she wanted to all-of-a-sudden write. My dad said, "I think it's a great idea. Go for it." One thing my mom is not and that's a procrastinator. After the bike ride, she practically threw her bike on the grass and ran upstairs to her desk to start on my book.

To make a really long story shorter, my mom wrote and published several books about Courtney and me—about our adventures. My life-of-Riley days are over. Now, it seems like I'm expected to make appearances in stores to meet people who want to buy my books. At first, I was really shy, but after three or four times, I got the hang of it. Kids love to hug me and I'm pretty good about posing for pictures. The flash is annoying, but I get extra dog bones on these particular days.

Did you know I've decided to have a career of my own? Yep, I created a syndicated column called "Just Ask Fraser," where dogs of all shapes and sizes get answers to their puzzling and heartfelt questions. I hate to interrupt my story, but I thought you might be interested in a letter or two.

Dear Fraser,

I'm troubled. I am a lovable bichon frisé named Sissy. I have been spoiled

by my human mom and dad since I was six
weeks old. We've been totally happy for
four incredible years. A week
ago, they arrived home with a
"baby." Now, I get no attention, hardly a morning petting. I've heard the stories
from fellow dogs but did I ever
in a million dog years believe it could
happen to sweet little me? Never. Please
HELP me.

                                    —Sissy
                        BOSTON, MASSACHUSETTS

Dear Sissy,

        All I can tell you is don't worry.
We've all been through it. It's a stage.
It won't last long. Take your mind off
your sadness. Best to "butter-up" to the
baby—look at it lovingly, stand over it
and really perfect your stance. Soon

you'll be the baby's irresistible protector and the attention you so desire will
return.

Here's to you,

—Fraser

Dear Fraser,

I'm a very well-taken-
care-of cocker spaniel. I have
a huge problem. My human
family just acquired a
Siamese cat named Psycho.
Must I say more? How can I
possibly co-exist with this
insane animal?

—Spunky

TOLEDO, OHIO

Dear Spunky,

Psycho will never change so sorry,
bud, but it's up to you. You must change

your attitude. Be grateful you have a
nice human family. Be grateful you have
plenty of food and a nice warm place to
sleep at night. So buck up—appreciate
what you have. My best advice to you is
to leave that dog-gone cat alone. Pay it
no attention and just watch what happens.
P.S. Let me know.

Fondly,

—Fraser

Dear Fraser,

I am a three-year-old black
Labrador named Black Sox.

I am not sure why I have that name
and my human dad, Mark, will not tell
me. Worse, he apparently has designated
me as the "official store greeter" at
his Cricket's Books and Gifts store here
in Sausalito, California. All day, I sit
in the store as customers arrive and

watch them look at books and gifts
including ones about dogs, and ugh, cats.

This might sound okay to you since
I do get petted sometimes, but the problem is that I am not paid anything for my
time except an occasional dog bone or two
or five. What I need to know is whether
there is minimum wage for dogs and how I
can find out what that is. Hopefully it
includes some cheese or tasty meat once
in a while since I get hungry just like
humans. Please help me.

Starving,

Black Sox

SAUSALITO, CALIFORNIA

Dear Black Sox,

I hear you, friend. If it makes you
feel any better, I don't get paid either.
Actually, it never occurred to me to pon-
der this issue before. But think about

it—it's not like you can go into a store
with your little doggie purse and the
people would figure out that you wanted
to buy something. Well, at least not in
our lifetime. Honor yourself and your
position at the store: you're with your
human dad, you get pets AND you get dog
bones. I'll have my mom call Mark and
tell him to feed you some cheese and
meat. How's that?

> Think gratitude and attitude,
>
> —Fraser

Dear Fraser,

My name is Mr. Jeepers. I'm a four-
year-old male terrier and I live on a
ranch in Woody Creek, Colorado. My human
parents have lots of animals besides me
and my two sister pooches, Flurry and
Mooney, and that's my problem . Now,
don't get me wrong, most of my fellow

creatures have their strong points: the peacocks have those big showoff tail feathers, the emus do this crazy dance with their long skinny legs, the roosters crow, the alpacas just stand around trying to look cute and, of course, Flurry and Mooney will do almost anything for a dog treat!

In my opinion, I'm the cutest, smartest and most well-behaved animal on the ranch! For some reason, my parents just don't always see it that way. They give corn to the birds, hay to the alpacas, and always give the exact same amount of food and love to all three of us dogs. What's the deal? I deserve better. I know more tricks and have perfected a certain perfectly quizzical head-cocked-to-the-side look that should guarantee an extra treat. So why, I ask, should I be considered a mere equal around here? Don't I deserve more? Fraser, you have books written about

you, so you must be quite brilliant.
You're my only hope. Please help.

Sincerely,

—Mr. Jeepers (your intellectual equal)

WOODY CREEK, COLORADO

Dear Mr. Jeepers,

What a coincidence, we're practically neighbors! I discussed your issue with
my human mom and she totally agrees with
how your human parents are handling the
situation. However, I agree with you,
man. So my mom and I have compromised—
every time she bakes my special treats,
Fraser's Favorites, we'll stop by, take
you aside and give you all the treats you
want. Sound fair? Looking forward to
meeting you.

Appreciate Your Life,

—Fraser

Stay tuned for more letters on page 107.

SCHOOL VISITS AND DOG BONES

I love my column. It keeps me busier than you'd expect. Just when I get the hang of writing my column and going into stores to boost sales of my mom's Fraser books, she adds a new twist. We now visit schools. My very first experience was in a 1st grade class. My mom told me I could stay in the car. She was going to read my book to the kids and then she'd come back for me so I could meet the children. Okay, that sounded fine as I attacked my newest chew toy. Awhile later, she returned and I proudly walked to school. I got within feet of the open classroom door and I smelled a scrumptious creature. I made a beeline for a large cage on the floor. YUM—a guinea pig—I couldn't believe my luck. What a great toy. Just as I poked my head into the cage, my mom grabbed me and dragged me outside. Next thing I knew, I had twenty-two kids surrounding me. It was pure chaos. I was overwhelmed by forty-four little hands "pawing" me. But, I took a few deep breaths, settled down and enjoyed all the attention. I could hear my mom and the teacher: "I'm so sorry," said the teacher, "I completely forgot about Jesabelle being in a topless cage on the floor. Please forgive me. I'm so glad you grabbed Fraser so quickly." My mom said, "Can you imagine the headlines of tomorrow's paper: 'Carnage in the Classroom'?"

Poor Jesabelle!

That was the first of many, many school visits. Now, my mom always checks the classroom first for

I love
school!

Jesabelles or baby chicks. Kids spend weeks watching their baby chicks hatch. One look at me, and those chicks would probably die of fright!

What's next? I know my mom wasn't through taking me places. I think secretly she wants her own adventures! Heck, there's even a song about me, "Fraser the Yellow Dog." Sometimes when we're in the car, it plays on the radio and my mom hums along. My mom can't stop writing—she has three more books in the works. I think she has a bit of an addiction.

I enjoy the process because she reads the rough drafts to me and I understand every word. I try to help her with the finer points: grammar, point of view and action. She listens to me so I take a lot of credit for these books being so popular.

Since my mom has an active mind, she can't seem to sit still. After the books came out, she decided kids needed a soft stuffed animal complete with my signature bandana. She got the Fraser dog made and I've only destroyed one or two. I like to play tug-of-war with them. As I just said, a cassette tape followed. My mom asked our neighbor, Polly, to write a song about me. Then she coaxed her friend, Bobby, into singing and recording it. A clothing line was next with adorable shirts, jeans and overalls with none other than my picture on them.

My mom's next project was the best of all, although to her it was a flop. She tested many varieties of dog bones and Abby and I got to try them out—some we liked better than others. We were in

doggie heaven. She picked my favorite recipe and called them Fraser's Favorites. I guess she miscalculated. There were too many other gourmet dog bones being sold so she ended up giving most of them away to our many dog friends. Fine with me—she has a huge jar with Fraser's Favorites so I never have to worry about running out of daily treats.

"A dog has one aim in life . . . to give you his heart."
—JOHN CAIRNS

DO I GET THE JOB?

Sure enough, my mom hasn't let down yet. One evening we drove to Snowmass to meet Rita. She's a real friendly lady in charge of the pet therapy program at our local hospital. She looked me over several times and then asked my mom to have me perform all the tricks I know: sit, stay, lie down, etc. I must have done a terrific job because Rita told my mom, "See you for duty Monday morning. Remember to give Fraser a bath. I'll meet you there for a run-through."

I forgot all about it and then a few days later,

my mom gave me an unexpected bath that felt great and off we went to the hospital. I walked in with my mom and Rita greeted us. She told my mom lots of information that I paid no attention to. The three of us went room to room and it's my job to get lots of pets and then lie quietly by the side of the patient's bed while my mom chats for a really long time with that person. The "patient" is usually on some kind of medication because they sometimes act kind of weird. Most of the adult "patients" leave their breakfasts untouched. I'm not supposed to but, heck, why not offer an always-hungry dog a piece of toast or some eggs once in awhile. I'm not complaining because the nurses give me plenty of bones, but still. . . .

I almost failed my test on that first day. Rita and my mom walked into Room 103. I followed until—halt—heck, no—linoleum floor. *NO WAY.* I'm not walking on that slick surface. I almost killed myself once and I immediately remember that experience. I stop suddenly and my mom is like, "It's okay, Frasie,

Oh no, linoleum floors are soooo slippery!

come on in." I can tell she's really embarrassed because her face turned as red as an apple. She started calling me all her favorite names and coaxing me in.

Uh uh, I'm not going. Then she and Rita tried the old dog bone trick, "Fraser, just come a little closer." I took two steps forward because I really wanted that bone. I stopped again and stepped back out onto the soft-carpeted hallway.

Rita said, "I'm sorry, Fraser would have been perfect."

Good, I think, I'm off the hook. However, my mom never gives up. "I've got an idea," she says and runs off to find some towels. She lays them down and I follow her, walking on the towels and not the linoleum. No problem. I can tell Rita's thinking really hard and finally she says, "Well, since we only have two rooms that aren't carpeted, if you bring in a folding rug, Fraser has the job."

By then, I've had my fill of dog bones and have decided that this job will actually be a lot of fun. We stood by the nurse's station and Rita said, "Good job, Fraser, you passed and are the newest pet therapy dog. You'll need to get your photo taken and it will be on the wall next to our other dogs. Here's your new collar, leash, dog badge and a t-shirt for your mom. Welcome to the hospital."

Okay, let's get outta' here. But no, we're walking down a path to another building. The Senior Assisted Living Center. Seems that after the rounds at the hospital, I still have more to do.

We went in and met Maggie and Connie who showed us a chart and where to go. My first "senior" I visit is Emma. She told us she's ninety-nine years old (I know lots of dogs that age, but not many

I adore my visits
with Emma.

people). I know this is a lady I'm going to love to visit. While Rita and my mom aren't looking, she sneaks me dog bones galore! In case I don't discuss this later in my book, I adore my visits to both the hospital and the senior center, but the best is visiting with Emma. Even Courtney comes with us sometimes. Emma has had her share of adventures and tells us lots of stories. I fall asleep but hear her in my dreams. To this day, she "over-treats" me!

Book signings, school visits, hospital and senior center visits—there's no rest for the good dog. I'm plum tired out. I wonder what's next?

"If you think dogs can't count, put three dog biscuits in your pocket, and try giving Fido two of them."

—PHIL PASTORET

BEARS IN MY HOUSE

All dogs that live in big cities are aware that bears exist. They hear about them from their dog friends and from their owners who relay stories like, "I'm taking the family camping. I just hope we don't see any bears." Word gets around about wild animals even though big-city dogs rarely see them. I really hadn't given it much thought either. Then, one summer, in our little town, berries were scarce and bears were seen everywhere, mostly ravaging for food in people's garbage cans or big dumpsters. One day, my mom and Courtney took Abby and me for an all-day hike in the mountains. We arrived home around 6:30 P.M. and I heard my mom tell Courtney, "That's weird, Dad's home. He's supposed to be sailing. I wonder what happened?" As my mom drove up to our house, she thought she saw my dad through the big kitchen windows on the second floor. It looked like he was lingering by the open refrigerator door contemplating what to eat. My mom pushed the button in her car that magically opens the garage door. It's always been a mystery to me as I'm usually pretty good about figuring things out.

"Dad's not home," cried Courtney. When my mom noticed his car was missing, she grabbed her cell phone and dialed 911. She frantically backed out of our driveway. I had no idea what was going on except that I knew I was starving. What? Where are we going? We were so close to getting dinner for me.

My mom drove as fast as she's ever driven to our friends' house, just down the road. As she's driving, she's talking on her cell phone, "Please come to 121

Daniel Drive. I think there's a burglar in my home."
My mom and Courtney are freaking out. I have no
idea what the big deal is—I just want my dinner.
While my mom was chatting with her friends, their
two sweet Samoyeds, Bear and Bugaboo, nicely share
their food with Abby and me. After our meal, we fall
sound asleep.

The police phone my mom and after a fairly
long conversation, she says to Courtney, "Wake up
the dogs, honey. We're going home. The good news
is there's no burglar, but the police told me we have

Busted!

Berries are fine, but this foie gras is delicious!

four bears in our house and it's a total mess."

Holy, doggie! As we drove in our driveway for the second time, there are six police cars greeting us with flashing red and blue lights. A nice policeman met us and he told my mom to keep Abby and me inside the car. Hey, what's up with that? I need to go potty. The policemen were still trying to get the bears out of the house with BB guns. We all watch, bewildered, as a mama and her three cubs are chased out of our house. Abby and I are barking like crazy from inside the car and those bears start running for the

45

woods behind our house. Forget the police; I would have had them out of the house in no time and with no guns.

We all went into the house and, oh mama . . . it smells like four bears and oh, oh, the entire kitchen is turned upside down. Cabinets are broken; the oven is open and scratched. Good for me, but bad for my mom and Courtney. Every item of food in the refrigerator and pantry is now on our wood floor. I'm just beginning to have a dog day helping with the clean up, when I hear my mom laughing hysterically and crying all at the same time. . . .

"It's okay, Mom," said Courtney, "I'll help you clean up." Then Courtney ran into her room and started crying, "Those bears were on my bed and ate all the candy I had stashed in my closet—you know the ones I saved for my friends at camp." My mom held me by my collar (Abby had stayed outside— she's always so wise). The three of us just stood there not believing our eyes. My mom started her meditation breathing in, out and in, out. That's when I know she's focusing. That's when I know she won't be agitated for long.

She told me to "stay" and she and Courtney went to work cleaning: cottage cheese, eggs, milk, sour cream, crushed vitamins, mashed fruits and vegetables, yogurt, rice, ground coffee, and the list goes on and on. The biggest problem is our wood floor, because all that stuff got caught in the space between the wood. It was a real mess. It took hours for my mom and Courtney to clean and the house still smelled awful. Bears smell terrible; worse than when I roll in horse poop. Bear smell was in the rugs and on the furniture, it was in the air. It was disgusting.

The excitement started to wind down around 11:30 P.M. Abby and I were especially tired due to all the commotion: strangers (policemen), intruders (four bears) and my family flipping out. Oh, and my dad arrived home around 10 P.M. after having a nice long dinner in a small town near the lake where he sails. When all this craziness began, my mom called him on his cell phone to report the bad news, but what could he do? He was an hour away. Seemed logical for him to eat and drink (rum and tonics are his drink of choice) while my mom and Courtney were frantically cleaning. Since I can't drive, I don't know what I would have done. Needless to say, when my dad walked through the door, my mom was not exactly happy with him. According to people law, he was not to receive any "good" points that night.

We all went to sleep. My dad came down to say good night to Abby and me and for some reason, he locked our front door and also locked the sliding glass doors next to where Abby and I sleep. About two hours into a great doggie dream where I'm on an amazing climb up a 20,000-foot mountain, all hell broke loose. Abby and I smell a bear and start barking like mad dogs. My dad wakes up from a deep sleep, dashes downstairs from his bedroom, runs out the front door like a wild man, flies through the garage door to the basement to retrieve his rifle. I was totally cracking up. Here he is, stark naked with his rifle in hand, pounding on our front door because it's locked and he can't get in. My mom comes downstairs and she's laughing at my dad. The bears are right behind him, probably coming back for round two. My mom opened the door quickly and my dad came in and shut the door. He ran to the phone, rifle in hand and called 911. Now all of a sudden, he's mad. He wasn't mad before. We live in an area where there are very few trees. My dad paid to have four crab apple trees planted in front of the house and the mama bear was climbing up one of these trees. Now that made him mad!

The 911 people said that there was nothing they could do. Having four bears in your house rates—you get seven policemen and six squad cars with flashing lights, but if you just have one bear attempting to break in, you're on your own. What are a dog and his family to do? Put up a dog gone good fight, that's what! And that's what we did. Abby and I barked incessantly while my dad went out on the deck and pounded his chest while making unusual screaming noises. He looked like a Neanderthal man. Things were really heating up! The bear looked at my dad like he was crazy (which he was) and decided to climb down and go somewhere else.

Well, at least for an hour or two. This game repeated itself again and again throughout the night. We barked, my dad did his Neanderthal man thing, the bear fled. . . .

Morning finally arrived. Abby and I went out for our run and NO BEARS. Inside our house, however, my family was still dealing with a yucky mess, a gross lingering smell and fear of the next bear break-in. To add insult to injury, all the windows needed to be closed tightly and all the doors had to be shut. The pungent bear smell got worse by the minute. During the day, the temperature got up to eighty-five degrees in the house. Abby and I luckily spent our time outdoors—guarding the house. Remember, no way those bears would have come inside in the first place if Abby and I had been home.

Sure enough, as soon as my family left, the four bears started down the mountain towards our house. Abby and I dashed over to the grove of trees where the bear family came to hang out waiting for their big chance at more food. We barked loudly and for a long time. We scared them and then they'd lumber back

Bear-free zone

up the mountain. This went on for days and, I must say, it screwed up our relaxing schedule, but we were happy to do our job. And a good one, at that! Five long days later, those hungry, annoying, smelly bears were gone. AMEN.

"You think dogs will not be in heaven? I tell you,
they will be there long before any of us."
—ROBERT LOUIS STEVENSON

DEATH AND DYING

I've heard about death before. Animals die all the time. One of my brothers died two hours after he was born. That's kind of the way it is—the circle of life and death in the animal kingdom. Survival of the fittest. I've heard all the buzz words about this major event. Never in a million years did I give it a thought until the fall of 1996. By then, I was two years old and Abby was nine. She was slowing down. God Bless her. She had a leisurely schedule: up at 8 A.M., an "older dog's" breakfast, a nap, a walk-run around our property, lots of water and a very long afternoon nap until dinner. I would usually tag along to keep her company. After her walk, her hip was extremely sore. My mom and dad were aware of this and didn't take her on long hikes anymore. Abby was mellow about her condition. She never complained. She just hung out and seemed to be happy to accept her fate. She got to the point where she didn't come up the twenty stairs to our house. She slept in the garage and I slept on a warm, soft bed next to her. We had long "chats" about life and how she appreciated hers and yet was ready to move on whenever our doggie God deemed it "her time."

Many evenings, she spoke quietly to me about death. She told me that death is a mystery and yet is no big deal because one day we all will die. I had never even thought that I might not be around for my daily walks. How could it be that one day I'd be gone and Courtney wouldn't have her Fraser to hug or throw tennis balls to? Abby told me the only important thing is to live life to its fullest. And I do.

I realized one day how lucky I was to be in the presence of this incredibly wise, elderly, beautiful dog that has passed on so much of her wisdom to me. She was always patient, especially when I was a pesky pup and then a wild and crazy teenager. Sadly, as days passed by, Abby lost her keen eyesight. I felt guilty as I went on my long runs alone, often thinking of her.

Many times when we went on walks together with my family, Abby would stumble and sometimes fall. Courtney spoke to her constantly so Abby would know where to go. One fall day, when the gorgeous weather beckoned my family and me to go on a long hike to a mountain lake through the most beautiful forest of aspen trees, my parents put Abby in the downstairs pen. They were scared she'd run off, fall down and get disoriented. So, off we went in the jeep for a very long drive to the trailhead. I love to go on hikes with my family. There are always new dogs to meet along the way as well as wonderful new sniffs. When my family hikes ten miles, I hike fifty!

We returned home many hours later, exhausted. All of a sudden, my mom jumped out of the car and screamed and then started wailing. Courtney started crying uncontrollably. My dad slowed the jeep and that's when I jumped out and ran to our pond. My family ran faster than I could ever have imagined.

Floating in the pond was our dear, sweet, beautiful Abby. Calmly, amid cries from Courtney and my mom, my dad waded into the pond and picked her up like he used to pick me up when I was a young pup. He carried her to our house. He felt her heart for any sign of life, and then did mouth-to-mouth resuscitation. He said a prayer and wrapped her up in a blanket.

I didn't know what to do. I knew her time was going to be up any day, but evidently my sad family did not. My mom and Courtney were sitting next to Abby's body, petting her on top of the blanket and telling her how much they loved her. All I could do was lick the salty tears off their heartbroken faces.

My dad was telling us that Abby dug a hole in the ground and escaped out of the pen. She then purposefully trotted down to the pond and ended her long, happy life. Dogs do that sometimes when we're ready to die. I already knew this—Abby told me.

My dad said, "Abby's spirit is gone—it's flown away. All that's left is her body. We'll bury her next to Chief, Scout, Brandy and Killy (my family's dogs who had died before Abby and I were born)."

Still sobbing, my mom ran upstairs and prepared for the burial. I'd never seen one before, but obviously, she'd been through a few. She gathered pictures of Abby, her favorite dog toys and her dog dish, her leash, her extra collar, all her medicines and a prayer book. Okay, that did it, now I'm so sad

Goodbye, Abby.

I can't even believe it.

My dad got his shovel. Now in the wild animal world, we die, we decompose and that's it. But in the people world, they do it differently. We all walked together up beyond the house to a clump of trees. There were four markers. It felt eerie being here. My dad started to shovel dirt. Normally, I would start digging, too. But instead, I lay down next to my mom and Courtney. It just felt like the right thing to do.

It took my dad a really long time to dig a deep hole in the ground. He gently placed Abby inside. My mom, dad and Courtney stood around the "grave" holding hands. I was very quiet as they talked to Abby. They told lots of stories—some I hadn't even heard before. She was one classy dame! My mom took out her spiritual book and everyone took turns saying their favorite prayer or poem.

Then they each shoveled some dirt back into the hole, covering Abby. My mom and Courtney petted me and watched as my dad shoveled the rest

I miss you...

of the dirt until the hole was gone. We all sat there in silence until the stars and moon came out. I wanted to "tell" them it was okay. I wanted to "tell" them that Abby knew she was near the end of her life and welcomed death. There were a lot of things I wanted to "say," but our communication skills don't cross over yet.

We walked back to the house. My mom made herself, my dad and Courtney mugs of hot chocolate and I forgot about my dinner. My dad made a fire and we all sat around it, feeling really helpless. They talked and cried. We all fell asleep on sleeping bags on the floor near the fireplace.

Until that day, I never knew how sorrowful

people could be. I knew I'd miss Abby a lot, but not like my family. In the days to come, things just weren't the same. My mom cried every time she came home. I even caught my dad crying in the garage. I tried to be happy with my other dog friends, but things were different for a very long time.

"Dogs are miracles with paws."

—UNKNOWN

MAGGIE

After Abby's death, I continued my routine with an occasional school visit, bookstore signing and weekly visits to the hospital. Things were "dog gone" good again. Life goes on. My family's happy spirits came back slowly but surely—thank "dogness!" Just when life was at its finest, things changed rapidly.

While pretending to sleep under the dinner table, but in truth waiting for crumbs to fall my way as they always do, I heard talk of getting a puppy. A five-letter word meaning a seven-letter word—

TROUBLE. Oh, I realize I was an adorable puppy once upon a time, but I'm grown now and only associate with wiser and more mature dogs. A puppy— are you kidding? I've gotten used to my obligations now; I'm happy, why ruin a good thing? My family has already forgotten the commitment of a puppy. It seems like fun and games at the time, but in truth, it's a pain in the rump: they consume your days and cry in the night. I'm resistant to change.

Our neighbors across the river, the Melbergs, have a very pretty, darker yellow Lab named Rosebud. From the name you would assume she's a spoiled princess, but when I met her, she was a tomboy and loved to explore. Rosebud was pregnant and my mom decided it was TIME.

You'd think my mom was preparing to give Courtney a brother or sister. All I heard for weeks was, "We need to get puppy gates for the kitchen. We need puppy chow. Let's go to the pet store and get one of those bears with a battery-operated heart-beat so the puppy won't miss its mom." And on and

Maggie

She looks cute now, but just wait...

on. It was really a bit nauseating. I still got plenty of attention, but I knew it was only a matter of time before my family's enthusiasm would turn into sleep deprivation. How did I know all this? Trust me; we dogs have an amazing network going. When we want an answer, we simply ask. Plus, Abby had filled me in on my own puppyhood.

The day finally arrived. I remember it well—the phone rang, Courtney answered and joyfully announced to my mom that Rosebud had delivered ten healthy puppies. My mom and Courtney threw on jackets and drove over to the Melberg's house leaving me at home to my own devices. They came home all chit chatty and at dinner, told my dad in detail about the birth of the tiny pups and Rosebud's extraordinary abilities of being the perfect mother. They spoke like there had never been a more amazing event. I was happy because Courtney snuck me a lovely piece of grilled steak. My dad and I shared similar views of this situation—WHATEVER! Luckily, I found out I had eight more weeks of grace because Rosebud needed to take care of the pups, feed them and teach them life's lessons. Yahoo! I counted my extra days and weeks of freedom with joy.

One afternoon, I came home from a glorious jaunt and there she was—a small puppy who looked just like me when I was that age. How did Rosebud produce a light-colored Lab like me? Evidently, this little pup was the only one that color in the litter and my mom picked her up immediately after birth and declared her, "the one."

"Fraser," cried Courtney, "come meet Maggie." So I pranced over and I must say she was quite adorable. She acted a bit dizzy as I watched her run down our steep hill. I knew she was getting used to her surroundings and would soon miss Rosebud and her littermates. Memories flashed back to me in waves. She ran over to me and started yapping and jumping around me, nipping at my leg. "Hey, toots, I'm not your mother. Get lost!" She continued to annoy me so I went into the garage for a nap.

After a short rest, I trotted upstairs to the kitchen and witnessed an amazing task in progress. "Hey Fraser," said my mom affectionately as she was preparing Maggie's dinner. I'm thinking, what's up with this? I couldn't believe my eyes; she actually put Maggie on her lap and spoon-fed the little princess. Next she'll be bottle-feeding her. That's when I knew

Are you kidding me?

I was in for some interesting times ahead. The next few weeks felt like a four-act play.

Act I. I went to bed as usual in my parents' room on my comfy doggie bed. Maggie settled down, as she was very tired from her first day away from her "original family." All was quiet and peaceful for one hour. Then, Maggie started crying and barking louder and louder, you know, that annoying, obnoxious puppy yapping. My dad went downstairs to the kitchen where Maggie was in her little box with her Rosebud-scented blankie and her battery-operated bear. Yeah, right. My dad took her outside to pee and baby-talked to her saying, "Good Maggie, now go back to sleep."

Needless to say, ten trips later (my mom and Dad took turns), dawn set in and my mom was so tired that instead of putting Maggie in her box, she put her on their bed where Maggie fell sound asleep in my mom's arms. She must have felt safe because she fell into such a sound sleep my mom actually had to wake her up in the morning. More spoon-

Maggie in a
kennel—piece
of cake!

feeding and tons of trips outside to relieve herself and be "trained" not to "go" in the house.

Act II. After three sleepless nights, I found my parents at the breakfast table reading up on kennel training. After hemming and hawing (this is what people do a lot of), they called Rosemary, my doggie doctor and consulted with her. Finally, it was decided—Maggie will be kennel trained. Let the games begin. Since I was traditionally trained, I'm anxious to see how this pans out.

Act III. My mom arrived home with two kennels—one for their room and one for the car. I love it. Maggie is put into the kennel (it's really a cage) in the car and instead of trying to bug me, she falls sound asleep.

At night, my family takes her for a short walk commanding Maggie to "hurry up," spoken quickly and with determination. This is another tidbit they recently learned. Then Maggie is transported (my parents carry her) upstairs into her bedroom kennel and falls asleep. She doesn't make a peep until 6:00 A.M. Hallelujah!! My family is well rested and in much better moods. I'm definitely passing this technique on to my doggie pals.

Act IV. It's only been a couple of weeks and my parents decide it's time for Maggie to stay at home with me. If Abby trained me, then their logic was I could train Maggie. Simple! My parents went to the market with Courtney one morning and I was left home with hyper Maggie who is cute, but always wanting to play and nip at my legs. I started to really appreciate Abby because I behaved in this

If Abby trained me, I can train Maggie.

exact manner. Okay, I rationalize, that was different; she was a "she"—a mother, a female, born and bred to take care of the young. Me, I'm a "he"—a man, a stud, not a father, not a teacher, nor a caregiver. They must have forgotten this fact. Perhaps my mom and dad will realize all this and turn around soon. Fat chance. I'll just have to make the best of an annoying situation. I've nicknamed Maggie "Little Pooper."

Truth be told, she's not too terrible. I got our schedule down to a science. As soon as our family takes off, I play the exceptional "role model" and run Little Pooper around the yard until she's exhausted and can't move another paw. I walk her over to her outside pen that my dad had to build because recently the coyotes in our neighborhood were killing puppies by the handful. This pen is like a fancy hotel equipped with a furry bed, a lovely water bowl decorated with Little Pooper's name and several paw prints, and puppy toys in every shape and size. I was surprised they didn't bother with a rose in a vase by her bed and a basket of fine soaps. Little Pooper slowly walks into the pen like a drunken sailor and takes a three-hour nap. That's when my work is done and I'm able to take off and run around the neighborhood for my morning visits.

P.S. Did I mention that my freedom was miraculously reinstated?

"If you pick up a starving dog and make him prosperous, he will not bite you. This is the difference between a dog and a man."

—MARK TWAIN

IS THIS REALLY FAIR?

What confuses me a little is that as much as I quickly enjoy my dog food; one cup in the morning and one cup in the evening (unless my dad or Courtney are feeding me and then I always get a bonus ½ cup), my parents linger over two and three hour dinners with their friends. They have little dinner parties that start around 6:00 P.M. This is just about the time I've inhaled my kibbles so I'm ready to hang around the house and rest. I enjoy these parties because I get a chance to greet their guests and I get plenty of pets.

I know most of them by now so I get extra attention for not barking!

These evenings start off with "cocktails" and four or five plates of absolutely yummy foods called appetizers. I know because when I was younger, I personally helped myself to every dish. I particularly liked the various cheeses. I must be fairly sophisticated because I found the "tartar" to be marvelous—very pleasing to my palate. After loads of laughter (we dogs crack up quite a bit, but we don't giggle and roar with laughter—it's just not our way), they sit down at the dining room table for more food. Boy am I jealous!

My dad goes outside to barbecue fish and meats and my mom steams veggies (yuck) and tosses a salad. They sit around the table for hours eating, drinking and constantly talking. At first I'm really into the whole evening because the guests are always sneaking me little bits of food, but when no more is offered, I'm bored and go to sleep under the table. I know I sound really spoiled and I suppose I am, but

How much do I enjoy my dinner?

come on—a few seconds to gobble down a measured portion of dog food versus two-hour meals? If I tried lingering over my food, Maggie would steal mine in a New York second. What's a guy to do?

In my next life, I'm going to choose to be my dad. Not only does he get to enjoy these long meals, but all I ever see him doing is mixing cocktails and sitting outside with his guy buddies flipping their food on the grill. Maybe someday I could try some of that rum he drinks. A "dogtail" might just loosen me up a bit!

P.S. Did I say what a total waste it is for my

mom to throw away all that perfectly good food that her guests leave on their plates? Why doesn't she throw it *my* way? Where's the consciousness?

"A dog wags its tail with its heart."

—MARTIN BUXBAUM

THE TALE OF MY TAIL

Have I mentioned yet what a conversation piece my tail is? Yep, not a day goes by that someone doesn't mention it.

"Now that's a tail."

"I can't believe how strong his tail is."

"That tail could really do some major damage."

"Owie."

"Ouchie wowa."

How would you feel if a part of your body caused these kinds of comments? I don't remember my tail being a problem until I turned two years old.

I must have really grown into my large-for-a-lab, 100-pound frame. Gosh, my whole body is big and strong, why shouldn't my tail follow suit?

My family became aware of it when our neighbor Kathryn called to ask my mom if she was sitting down. I knew it—she was telling my mom how I had entered her house through her doggie door and before she could grab me, my tail had whacked her $1,000 14th-century Chinese vase off her coffee table in one fell swoop. I could tell my mom was horrified.

"Of course we'll pay you back," she said reluctantly.

"HO, HO, HO." Kathryn was cracking up with laughter.

"What's so funny?" asked my mom.

"That vase was a gift from my ex–mother-in-law and I've always hated it. Fraser's done me a huge favor. HO, HO, HO."

Relieved, my mom came over to me and I let my tail go crazy, as usual. She wanted to see exactly how my tail could have performed this vase-whacking maneuver.

"Ow, Fraser, your tail does hurt," said my mom.

One day it wasn't an issue, and the next that's all anyone talked about. Seems like every day after that little event, my family discussed my tail.

"I'll move all the pictures off the coffee table," said Courtney.

"Yeah and no more placing flowers on that table, either," said my mom.

Soon, all the tables I could easily reach were bare.

My dad said, "When we put up the Christmas tree, we can't put ornaments on the lower branches."

My mom said, "I just hope he doesn't knock the tree down."

Phone calls were made to all of our neighbors to warn them of my newest weapon of destruction. Many neighbors boarded up their doggie doors in fear of what my tail might do. The neighbors who really love me simply removed everything off of their

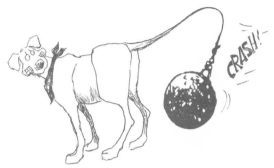

When did my tail become so powerful?

low tables.

I felt different. I felt a little special that everyone was going to so much trouble for me, but in a different way than before. I tried so many times not to wag my tail, but I couldn't stop it no matter what.

Oh well, I just decided to accept this difference and make the best of it. I did have a few bloody days ahead that I never anticipated coming. If I whacked it hard enough, it would bleed. And I mean bleed everywhere. My mom tried putting a big bandage on with lots of tape, but it slipped off after a few minutes. Luckily, my family loves me so much they just cleaned up the blood and told me they were sorry for me. I now lick my tail the best I can until it quits bleeding.

One time, my mom and I were working at the hospital and a maintenance man told the nurse, "We have a problem, there's blood all over the walls and floor near Room 104." My mom heard the man, looked at my tail and sure enough, the mysterious blood was coming from me. My mom admitted to the nice man where the blood came from. First he couldn't believe it, but then he felt so bad that he gave me lots of treats and cleaned up my blood. If I could have spoken, I would have thanked him. But I think he knew.

The only other problem my tail has caused is when I go into stores for book signings. My mom has to be really careful that no books are propped up on a table, or else. . . . One time I went into a kitchen shop where they sell my books and oops, a whole stack of china plates went flying. Bummer, there went all the profits!

Crazy as it may sound, kids actually put their faces in the line of fire because for some reason they enjoy getting whacked. GO FIGURE.

Fig. 1

Fig. 2

"A dog is a smile and a wagging tail. What is between doesn't matter much."

—CLARA ORTEGA, *DOG QUOTATIONS*

MY TAIL PART II

I recently had a fairly devastating episode occur. My parents were out of town and one of my favorite dog sitters Jeremy was staying at our home. It was June—I know this significant fact because the bears were out of their winter slumber and had been making nightly visits.

One night, Jeremy went out on the town looking for some fun and left Maggie and me home with the garage door closed so the bears couldn't get inside and eat our precious dog food or get into the garbage. Jeremy left a very small insulated cooler outside to dry. He had washed it out earlier in the day.

10:00 P.M.: Enter a humongous black bear. He opened the door, bold as all get-out. Maggie and I are barking as hard and loud as we possibly could. This bear then lumbered over to the porch stairs and spotted the cooler.

I'm so excited. My body takes over in these instances. Every cell feels danger. I possess complete knowing. I immediately go into protective mode. That is to say I will not allow any stranger to enter into my beloved territory. I, like all dogs, took a vow when I was old enough to be the protector. People think we dogs just bark, but that's not completely true, we put out an energy, a vibe, a distraction that says to any intruder, "Get out." I've scared away a lot of people and critters in my day but this particular bear was hungry, large and nothing I did seemed to deter him from grabbing that cooler.

My tail was wagging harder than ever and suddenly—wham, ouch, whew, I'm hurt. No, not by the bear who has taken off with the cooler, but for some reason, my tail is bleeding and hurts like crazy. Damn, I sliced it again but I think I sprained it, too. I try as hard as I can to wag, but my tail hangs limp.

Jeremy arrives home soon after and lets Maggie and me into the house. He pets us both and asks how we are. He notices right away that I'm in pain. "Fraser, what's wrong, boy?" he asks.

He calls the vet and off we go in the car late at night. We go to a new vet—someone I don't know. She seems likeable and reassuring at first. She bandages my tail but then she tapes my tail to my leg. Are you kidding me, lady? Do you realize how humiliating this is?

Obviously not. I'm a grown dog with a taped tail. I tried wagging my tail and all that happened was that my body wiggled. This is not going to work. We drove home. I didn't feel so good. They'd given me some pills that made me feel "out of it." My senses were dulled and I was sleepy. I slowly got up onto my sleeping couch and conked out until the next morning.

NO WAY...I want
to keep my tail!

Slowly I opened one eye and then the other. I walked gingerly down the stairs to the lawn to pee. Now I have to poop. Have you ever tried to poop with a sprained tail that's taped to your leg? Bet you didn't know that we dogs use our tails to help us poop. I let Jeremy know that I was not a happy boy. Jeremy felt so sorry for me that he called my parents. My dad told him to un-tape my tail. He did, and thank goodness for small acts of kindness.

I healed after five weeks but there is talk that if this happens again, they might have to amputate the tip of my tail. I've got news for them—NO WAY.

"A faithful friend is the medicine of life."

—PROVERB

HOW WOULD YOU FEEL?

One day I was running really hard with my mom and dad. They were riding their mountain bikes up a very long hill by our house. The road was winding with lots of dips. We stopped at a cool pond where I swam for a long time. Then back on the road after a snack. After a fun loop, we had a long downhill back to our house. I took a long nap and when I woke up, I was very sore—which I'm usually not! After my dinner, I went upstairs to my soft dog bed, and fell sound asleep until the next morning.

I woke up because I really had to pee. I stood up and yow-wee! My right knee felt weird, a feeling I've never had before. It was sort of painful, but the feeling perplexed me. It kind of took my breath away—like would it hold up if I walked on it? I wasn't so sure. I slowly went upstairs and nudged my dad to let me out. Instead of barreling outside to chase bunnies and chipmunks, I slowly went down the two flights of stairs. I peed on the closest bush and walked gingerly around the yard. How did I feel? Weird. I just couldn't trust my right knee to hold me up; it felt like it might just collapse. After just a short walk, my knee did collapse a few times. I have to admit, I was concerned.

When my mom asked, "Do you want to go for a run, Frasie?" I knew I did, so as usual, I forgot about my knee and ran like crazy and felt good. But after the run, my leg hurt so badly that I had to take the weight off of it. For the first time in my life, I began to limp.

My mom knew right away something was

wrong so she carried me into the car and we drove an hour away to our holistic veterinarian. Dr. Ron weighed me and checked my entire body using his hands and a few instruments that were cold and felt great. I was tired and my mom kept petting me so I felt nice and relaxed. Dr. Ron said, "I think Fraser has torn his ligament. Unfortunately, this kind of injury needs time to heal. You're going to have to let Fraser rest. You can't take him running for a few weeks."

Excuse me, I'm thinking, not run for a few weeks? I heard my mom cry. She told Dr. Ron, "You don't understand, Fraser loves to run. If he doesn't run, he'll go crazy."

I knew she was on my side! Dr. Ron said, "I know it's hard, but if you don't take the time to let him heal, he'll get worse and may end up needing surgery. Then he'll really go crazy. Talk to him, give his body lots of massages and pet him. Keep him on a leash when he goes outside or keep him in the house. I have some supplements and homoeopathics

I love to run.

to give him that'll help his healing. Good luck."

I could tell my mom felt bad. She talked to me all the way home. "Gosh, Frasie, I guess I'll have to read to you and play soft healing music." I thought, "I will go nuts unless I run. Woe is me. Why can't I run? It's what I do. Not run? They might as well shoot me. Okay, I'll try and be good. I'll try and be patient and think good thoughts. I'll try and eat that yucky medicine—but it won't be fun. Why me? What did I do to deserve this? Maggie can still run and play—why can't I? I don't wish this on Maggie or Scratchy, but why not some creepy, mean mongrel? I'm a good boy. I'm kind and sweet. AND I LOVE TO RUN. BUMMER. Real bummer."

Then I got real scared. I got mad, angry, irritated. Give me a break. I tried really hard every day to think good thoughts but when my mom took Maggie for a run and I had to stay home, it drove me nuts, crazy, ballistic...I was left in the house and because I was so bored, I started ripping my bed apart. When my mom returned home, she quietly collected the chunks of bed stuffing that I had deposited all over the living room. Instead of yelling at me, she sat me down, petted me, and sweetly said, "It's okay, Fraser, you're going to be fine. You're such a good boy." She said really nice things to me over and over. Day after day, when my mom and Maggie went out for a run, I could hear my mom's voice travel throughout my body and soul telling me that I'm okay, I'm good and pretty soon, I started to believe it.

I quit shredding my bed and lying around

feeling sorry for myself. I started concentrating on my breathing. Instead of feeling anxious, I felt better, more relaxed. I stretched my "good" legs over and over to keep them strong. I had long conversations with Scratchy because after all, she lived in the house and I figured I might as well take advantage of my time with her. Why waste the day? Scratchy started teaching me lots of lessons she had learned throughout her life. She told me wonderful cat stories. She told me that cats have nine lives—wow that's pretty cool. If you screw up one, you still have eight left to redeem yourself.

She told me the sad story about the day she was taken from her cat mom and family. It was a lot like my story. She told me how lucky she was to be picked by our human family because they lived nearby. Our mom would sometimes drive her over to visit with her cat mom and the family that raised her from a tiny kitten. All the kids would get so excited. Courtney and their daughter, Dylan were good friends so it all worked out great.

Scratchy's big thing is catnip. She gets "high" every day and it takes the edge off life when it seems unfair. I asked her if I could try some, but she told me it only works for cats. Too bad for me, it sounded like a great way to escape for a while. After her catnip "high" she would lie down for hours in the sunshine and be as "happy as a clam."

Instead of a cat bed, she's allowed free access to our house—except the kitchen counters and the dining room table. Not me. I'm not allowed on the couches or the beds. Truthfully, it's fine with me

Scratchy flying
high on catnip.

because otherwise I get way too hot.

These chats with Scratchy have been very cool because I can really spill my heart out to her. Maggie's never had anything wrong with her so she totally doesn't understand. Scratchy lets me be who I am. Plus I never took the time to find out how amazing she is—and after her catnip, who knows what words of wisdom will come out of her mouth? I thought about teaching her my breathing techniques, but I don't see the point. She's already so chill.

I think my knee feels better because I have Scratchy's company. Also, my mom and dad and Courtney pet me more and are always talking so kindly to me. I look forward every day to running again but for now I think I'm okay.

Day after day I grow stronger in my heart and soul. I get kind of used to hanging around the house resting and doing my little exercises. Scratchy put things into perspective—she told me it could be worse—I could have had surgery where they cut you and afterwards you're drowsy, sore and not able to run for months. I held onto that thought.

Several weeks later my mom carried me to the car and drove me back to see Dr. Ron. I had to wait in the front waiting room with four cats in cages, a huge St. Bernard, a golden retriever with a cast on his left leg, a tiny white fluffy "thing" that looked like a huge rat and a Jack Russell terrier who was panting and wanted to be out chasing a ball. Except for the Jack Russell, they all looked kind of scared or else really bored. I couldn't tell for sure. I felt a bit nervous.

It seemed like I had to wait forever for my turn. All the moms and dads sat around and either chatted about us and our problems or read magazines. The nurse finally called, "Fraser, come on in." I looked at my mom and she took me by my leash and led me in the white room with the metal table. I started to shake because I remembered that's where the doctor had given my mom the bad news about me not being able to run. I took a deep breath and let Dr. Ron carry me onto the table. He listened to my heart and then gently felt my knee. I didn't yelp like I had before. He smiled at me and told me I must have been a very patient boy because my knee was almost all healed. He told my mom that now I could start off going for very short runs and within a couple of weeks, I'd be back to normal.

I couldn't believe my ears. What he said was the best news I had ever heard. I smiled and smiled. I was so happy and couldn't wait to get home and tell Maggie and my newest best friend, Scratchy, the great news.

I guess I want all my fellow dog friends everywhere to know that there's always hope and when life throws you a curve ball, sometimes you just have to catch it and go for the ride. Life isn't always easy or fair but it sure is interesting. Make the best of each and every day. You never know what's around the bend.

"A dog is the only thing on earth that loves you more than he loves himself."

—JOSH BILLINGS

OUR SUNDAY ADVENTURE

People, I've learned are creatures of habit and my parents are no exception. Me, I can eat anytime of the day or sack out whenever I get a chance, anywhere. But my parents, now there's another story. My parents wake up and go to sleep pretty much the same time every day. They eat the same kinds of food items over and over—so do I but that's because I have no choice in the matter. They drive the same cars, go to work, and do the same sports over and over. They chat with the same

Everything including the kitchen sink!

people. Come on—dear, sweet parents, change it up a bit.

Oh, and every Sunday in the winter, they pile Maggie and me into the big car loaded with skis, poles, boots, hats, gloves, sunglasses, neck gators, jackets, scarves, backpacks, water bottles, leashes and lots more gear. We barely fit in the back! We drive for a long time—Maggie and I catch up on some sleep and then boom—we're there. Yep, the same parking spot each week. Happily I have to admit I love these Sunday winter outings. I actually look forward all week to them. First of all, I get to run and run. Then unbeknownst to my parents, people we meet along the way sneak us treats without even asking!! I love the wonderful sniffs and best of all—real live horses!

My parents and Courtney cross-country ski to a popular mountain eatery and Maggie and I run along. Because people are either lazy or don't know how to cross-country ski, the restaurant provides an old-fashioned sleigh pulled by two huge horses. The very first time we went up there, I spotted those horses and Maggie and I raced over to bark at them to let them know who was boss. Then I heard my parents yelling for me—like I've done something bad. Hey, what about Maggie? My dad jumps out of his skis and runs after me as fast as he can. He grabs my collar and puts me on a leash. Well, at least I made it perfectly clear to those horses that I'm a force to be reckoned with! The sleigh is long gone so my dad takes the leash off and Maggie and I run all over diving into snow banks and generally having a great time.

I smell the horses nearby. My parents grab Maggie and me and put us back on our leashes. Sure enough, the horses are standing at the entrance to the mountain restaurant. I trot as close to them as I can and start barking. I want them to remember me. All of a sudden, I get a rush of emotion—I feel sorry for those poor horses. They're tied up to a post and they have blinders on. I hate to be tied up and I think having big shields over my eyes would be a real drag. You couldn't look around. I appreciated being a dog.

We have to wait outside while my family goes in for one of those long people lunches. Little do my parents know that the chef comes out and gives Maggie and me a special treat—meat or chicken. What a nice dude! Also the little kids who come to the restaurant get bored eating with their parents so they come outside to play with us. My parents always finish their lunch before the sleigh leaves and takes the non-skiers back to their cars. So I get one more chance to walk by the horses and have a little chat.

Giddyup!

I strike up a conversation with one of the horses. Her name is Daisy and quickly she tells me that she and Dapper have this sleigh-gig for six months every year. They get fed really well, only have to work two hours a day, get lots of rest and meet tons of dogs. Their boss doesn't get it—Daisy and Dapper love dogs and enjoy talking to them but their boss and the dog owners freak out every time. Oh, well, we have a nice chat and I say, "See you in a few minutes."

My parents take off skiing and Maggie and I run

down the hill—fast. Then all hell breaks loose. Maggie is rolling over and over in horse poop, the sleigh goes by, I'm barking to say "hi" to my new horse friends and my parents are jumping out of their skis and grabbing us. The sleigh driver is yelling and out of nowhere a blinding blizzard blows in. It's bedlam. I'm delighted—I love it when it snows.

This is just a typical Sunday adventure. I learned something from the horses today. Listen to others. You may think one thing but you may be pleasantly surprised to find out that what you originally thought was true isn't. Oh and by the way, I'll never be a creature of habit—never.

P.S. Thirteen is a lucky number for me. Even though I have new adventures every day, my editor suggested I end my stories with this chapter. Okay, so my stories are over, but I have some interesting information and a quiz to share. Read on.

"The greatest pleasure of a dog is that you may make a fool of yourself with him, and not only will he not scold you, but he will make a fool of himself too."

—SAMUEL BUTLER

DID YOU KNOW?

From what I've heard (and now I'm a man around town), dogs are ever so popular these days. I'm listing some facts I find fascinating. Did you know?

Canine CPR classes are available? Be a responsible dog owner.

You can hire a "pet nanny," a dog walker or simply take us (no, not me) to doggie day care?

There are doggie spas and full-service resorts sprouting up all around the country? Our human families have choices now—send us to a kennel or—and I repeat or—send us to a spa complete with our own room, massages, better food and snacks, our own personal dog walkers, plus, they allow us to bring our own dog beds. Trust me, fellow dogs, being pampered is the way to go.

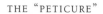

THE "PETICURE"

DID YOU KNOW?

There are do-it-yourself dog washers?
Our human families can give us a
bath without ruining their bathtubs.

*There are artists who
paint our portraits? Yep,
they'll paint a picture of
us on plates, mugs,
lamps, tables—the list is
endless.*

*Dogs are being
trained to be
chemical detectors
and work alongside
police-trained dogs to
sniff out narcotics?*

*You humans can hire a "poop buster" to clean up
your yard after us? Just think, no more weekends
spent cleaning our poop!*

We have animal welfare lawyers?

Doggie cookbooks are available so we can finally get some decent home cooked meals?

There is a dog museum in St. Louis, Missouri? I told you we're special!

We have our own specialized dog shops? There you can purchase: gourmet bones, a variety of leashes and collars, cool toys, outrageous clothing outfits, personalized dog dishes, picture frames, tons of books about us, dog jewelry and bumper stickers. My personal favorite bumper sticker reads: "MY LAB IS SMARTER THAN YOUR HONOR STUDENT."

Most cities have doggie parks so that city dogs can socialize with other dogs? Humans can bond with other humans.

City dogs can be tattooed or fitted with an I.D. microchip that can be scanned?

Many churches offer blessings upon us?

There are no bad dogs? Thank goodness Mrs. Woodhouse finally told the world.

There is now a doggie beauty pageant? I'm a little worried about the message here. Don't people realize we're all beautiful in our own way?

We're helping the war on terrorism?

*We have our own clubs, websites, TV shows
and movies? Remember guys; I'm patiently
waiting for my movie!*

*There are doggie toothbrushes with
special toothpaste?*

*The word "Dog"
is "God" spelled
backwards?*

*If you give us a human name, it means you
tend to hold us in high regard?
Thanks, Mom, Dad and Courtney!*

DID YOU KNOW?

Did you know that we have choices when it comes to health care? Yes, from acupuncture, massage, bio energetic medicine to chiropractic and animal massage therapy.

In Europe, we dogs are not only allowed, but welcomed in most restaurants?

There are dog psychics?

The Aspen Recreation Center has a Doggy Swim Day at the pool from time to time?

A note from Fraser: I accept letters all week long. My mom and I read each and every word. I'm a bit limited for space, so if I don't print your letter, I'll be sure to send you a response through the mail. Be strong dog fellows.

Dear Fraser,

I'm a standard female poodle and lead a very sheltered life. My mom, Phyllis, is in her 60's and has some social issues. I like to go out for long walks and yet she insists on very short walks.

She talks on that silly telephone speaking into the air. She rambles on and on
about not wanting to walk past a certain
house because "a single man" lives there
and might notice how "old" she looks.
Instead, she walks the other way. That
"man" happens to have an incredibly handsome male poodle—just my size! What
should I do? I'm hoping we could kill
three birds with one stone: I could hook
up with that stud of a poodle, she could
talk to a real person and my walks could
increase substantially.

—Addie

INDIANAPOLIS, INDIANA

Dear Addie,

You're going to have to be sensitive
to your mom's "getting older" issues. Try
this: the next time she takes you for a
walk, simply start walking in the oppo-

site direction. Pull if you need to. You
must retrain her to walk by the man's
house. Trust me, when she walks by the
"man's" house and he comes out and
starts flirting with her, she'll quickly
forget her age-worries and she'll flirt
back. Meanwhile, you and the "stud" can
get to know each other. You'll get her
on a schedule, you'll walk further, you
can both flirt and you'll both be happi-
er. It's what humans call a win-win situation!

> All the Best of Luck,
>
> —Fraser

Dear Fraser,

I'm a real fan of yours. I love your
amazing column. I can't bear it another
minute. People don't think we dogs know
what DIVORCE is. But we do. The two kids
in our family go for "counseling" to

discuss their
pain over our
mom and dad
divorcing. Hey,
what about me? I
have deep feel-
ings and emotions. It

just about tears me apart when my dad
comes on Sundays to pick me up for a
"visitation." I need a good dose of
therapy and some extra treats to help me
feel better. However, both my divorced
parents are clueless—they're only thinking about themselves, the children and
something called "money."

—Sly

CHICAGO, ILLINOIS

Dear Sly,

I feel for you, friend. I definitely
think you should insist upon therapy with

the best therapist. Grab a phone book, drop it onto the floor, and find "Dog Psychologists" in the yellow pages. Lie down next to the phone book and wait. Whine if you need to. Trust me; you'll get your point across.

You'll be fine,

—Fraser

Dear Fraser,

I am really quite famous. My name is Jersey and two years ago I was stolen when I was quite young and soon after, returned to my freaked-out family. While in captivity, I made the front cover of the Vancouver Times and my story was on radio and television. Recently, I met your human mom and dad at my family's B & B. They told me about you and your column so I'm writing to ask one question. I'm an American Staffordshire bull

terrier and we are well known to sleep
with humans on their beds. Yes, we like
the sheets over us. In my case, because
of my past trauma, I insist on sleeping
between my mom and dad on "our" bed. I've
been hearing talk that my parents are
trying to break me of this "habit." I've
heard that they may buy me a very com-
fortable bed of my own with my name
embroidered on it. But the bed will be
placed on the floor. Away from my place
on our bed? Why change something that's
been working so well? After all I went
through, don't I deserve the very best?
What should I do?

—Jersey

SALT SPRING ISLAND, B.C., CANADA

Dear Jersey,

What an amazing story. I'm so glad
you were returned safely. Yes, you do

deserve the best. Frankly I personally
get way too hot on a bed, but I respect
our differences. My **advice** to you is:
let them get you a bed with your name on
it but never, ever lie down on it. Just
keep going to your "spot" on "your" bed.
Give them "the look." I will assure you
that they will feel so sorry for you
they'll never kick you off. Be strong.
Persevere.

Keep me posted,

—Fraser

"If you are a dog and your owner suggests that you wear a sweater, suggest that he wear a tail."

—FRAN LEBOWITZ

LAB FACTS—DOS AND DON'TS

Note from Fraser: In case I've inspired any of you readers to choose a Labrador retriever to be a member of your family, there are a few things you should know about our breed first.

1. Do love me.

2. Do buy me gourmet dog bones.

3. Don't adopt me if you love the color black. Or, at least be forewarned: your black clothing will be covered with my dog hairs.

4. Don't buy me Burberry or Harley Davidson outfits. I like to go naked. If you're into designer clothing, consider a smaller breed or a lap dog.

5. Do know that furniture is an issue. Buy tan or beige. If you have dark-colored furniture, your guests will end up standing their entire visit, or they'll be wiping dog hairs off and look annoyed.

6. Do brush me daily.

7. Do go to your local butcher and ask for leftover bones or scraps.

8. Do get "doggie" bags from restaurants whenever possible. It's better to feed me leftovers than for you to overeat.

9. Don't put ribbons of any kind in my hair.

10. Don't paint my toenails (Okay, I won't speak for the gals).

11. Don't place a barking collar on me. I bark for a reason.

12. Don't fence me in unless the fence is enormous. I love my freedom too much.

13. Do have me jog at least twenty to thirty minutes a day, or let me run free. Hopefully, you'll have dog-loving neighbors like we do.

14. Do make sure I have lots of contact with people, especially with children, as well as other dogs.

15. Do play nice music.

16. Do know that I'm fearless. The exceptions are fireworks and thunder—they tend to freak me out.

17. Do read to me so I can expand my vocabulary. I'm capable of speaking several languages without enrolling in Berlitz!

18. Do allow me to swim, as I love the water.

19. Do know that if you listen, I can communicate with you.

20. Do take lots of photos, as I'm extremely photogenic.

21. Do have a strong arm if you want to adopt me because you'll be throwing millions of balls or Frisbees.

22. Don't forget, I'm a retriever—as in I love to chase and retrieve so beside round objects that are thrown into the air, I also enjoy food thrown my way. I can retrieve in mid-air which is a great crowd pleaser.

23. Do know I have a huge heart.

24. Do know I have so much love to give.

"If your dog thinks you are the greatest person in the world, don't seek a second opinion."

—JIM FIEBIG

TRUE OR FALSE?

Here's a little quiz for all you humans. Kids and adults, feel free to do this together. It'll be fun. Check for the correct answers on page 122.

1. The longer a dog's nose, the more well developed the dog's sense of smell.

☐ True ☐ False

2. Dogs have fifty teeth. ☐ True ☐ False

3. It is actually muscles in the skin that allow our dog hairs to stand up. ☐ True ☐ False

4. Dogs sweat through our paw pads.
☐ True ☐ False

5. Dogs see only in black and white.
☐ True ☐ False

6. Dalmatian puppies are born with black spots.
☐ True ☐ False

7. The oldest documented dog's life was twenty-nine years. ☐ True ☐ False

8. My breed, a Labrador retriever is the most popular dog in the U.S.A.
☐ True ☐ False

9. If dogs are fighting, use your bare hands to break up the fight. ☐ True ☐ False

10. We dogs have an easier time identifying a single-syllable name over a multiple-syllable name. ☐ True ☐ False

11. Dogs only growl when we're angry or threatened, not when we're playing.
☐ True ☐ False

12. Dogs sleep approximately fourteen hours a day. ☐ True ☐ False

13. It's inhumane to crate-train a puppy.
☐ True ☐ False

14. The smallest breed of dog is a chihuahua.
☐ True ☐ False

15. The best time to adopt a puppy is during the fourth week of life. ☐ True ☐ False

16. Humans should establish themselves as the dog's alpha. ☐ True ☐ False

From *The Dog Owner's Manual*, by Dr. David Brunner and Sam Stall, Quirk Books, Philadelphia, PA. ©2004.

True or False Answers

1. True
2. False. Dogs have forty-two teeth.
3. True
4. True
5. False. Dogs do see in color—just not as vividly as humans.
6. False. Dalmations are born pure white.
7. True. It was an Australian cattle dog or "blue heeler" from Queensland in northeastern Australia.
8. True
9. False
10. False. Thanks, guys, for naming me Fra'·ser.
11. False
12. True
13. False. Be sure to crate-train properly.
14. True
15. False. Puppies younger than eight weeks should not be separated from their families.
16. True

Okay, let's see how you did on the True or False quiz!

YOUR SCORE!

    1–4   questions answered correctly
          = "Paper Trained"

    5–8   questions answered correctly
          = "Chewing Controlled"

   9–12   questions answered correctly
          = "Comes When Called"

 13–16   questions answered correctly
          = "Best-of-Show"

CREDENTIALS

Just in case you thought I was making all these stories up, I thought I'd set the record straight and show you some of my credentials. . . .

Yes, this is
the real me, Fraser,
patiently waiting to
visit a school.

I told you my fans
like to "paw" me.

WILDWOOD SCHOOL. ASPEN CO

My mom and I after a
school visit
in Denver with
Colorado
Avalanche
hockey player,
Rob Blake.

READ TEAM. 2003

"Outside of a dog, a man's best friend is a book; inside of a dog it is very dark."

—GROUCHO MARX

THE TAIL END OF THE TALE

In conclusion, I've had a blast writing my story. I urge all my fellow canines to do the same. Pass on the lessons to the next generation.

In case you forgot my introduction, I still think my movie is right around the corner. Faith in a good life lived well opens doors. Go through those doors and you, too will realize your dreams.

Okay, so much for my sentimental side, I know you want to hear what my next book will be. *The Game of Golf According to Fraser* could be a hit. Stay tuned . . .